DOTZ
Goes to Camp

Jason Bretzmann
Illustrated by Melanie Davis

For Jack and Cooper, the original Dotz and Poo Poo. And for their amazing mom, Chris Bretzmann.

-Jason

For MC—even artists need a coach.

-Melanie

ISBN: 978-0-578-66492-7

Printed in the United States of America

The Bretzmann Group, LLC

Dotz was a very smart animal. He was best at two very important things.

He was best at making decisions.
And he was best at learning things.

He knew that these were two of the most important things that anybody could do.

Dotz was happy because it was summer. The weather was nice and he could play outside all the time.

Dotz was excited that his family signed him up for soccer camp.

At soccer camp there were lots of kids and lots of balls and lots of distractions.

Dotz knew it would be difficult to listen to his coach the whole time. He would have to really focus on making good decisions.

Dotz knew he wanted to learn more about playing soccer and this was a great time to do it.

Dotz listened to his coach and practiced dribbling.

Dotz listened to his coach and practiced passing.

Dotz listened to his coach and practiced shooting. He decided it was going to be a fun day of learning!

After awhile Dotz and the other campers started to get silly.

They started to try to make each other laugh instead of listening to their coach.

Dotz knew he had to make a decision. He asked himself, "Was it time to be silly? Or was it time to listen and learn?"

Dotz decided it was time to listen and learn from his coach. This was a good decision.

He learned so much.

He learned to dribble.

He learned to pass, he learned to shoot,
and he scored lots and lots of goals.

Everybody cheered a lot for Dotz because he made a good decision. Everybody cheered a lot for Dotz because he had learned so much.

Everybody cheered a lot for Dotz
because he scored a lot of goals.

Dotz was very happy he made a good decision and Dotz was very happy he learned so much.

Even so, he would have to make more decisions and learn more tomorrow because it was getting late and it was time for bed.

Good night Dotz. Good night everybody.